PARKER TAKES A TRIP

by **Parker Curry & Jessica Curry**
illustrated by **Brittany Jackson & Tajaé Keith**

Ready-to-Read

Simon Spotlight

New York   London   Toronto   Sydney   New Delhi

For Lia
—P. C.

For Papi & Nana
—J. C.

SIMON SPOTLIGHT
An imprint of Simon & Schuster Children's Publishing Division
1230 Avenue of the Americas, New York, New York 10020
This Simon Spotlight edition December 2024
Text copyright © 2024 by Parker Curry and Jessica Curry
Illustrations copyright © 2024 by Brittany Jackson
All rights reserved, including the right of reproduction in whole or in part in any form.
SIMON SPOTLIGHT, READY-TO-READ, and colophon
are registered trademarks of Simon & Schuster, LLC.
Simon & Schuster: Celebrating 100 Years of Publishing in 2024
For information about special discounts for bulk purchases, please contact Simon & Schuster
Special Sales at 1-866-506-1949 or business@simonandschuster.com.
The Simon & Schuster Speakers Bureau can bring authors to your live event. For more information
or to book an event contact the Simon & Schuster Speakers Bureau at 1-866-248-3049
or visit our website at www.simonspeakers.com.
Manufactured in the United States of America 0325 LAK
2 4 6 8 10 9 7 5 3
CIP data for this book is available from the Library of Congress.
ISBN 978-1-6659-4282-9 (hc)
ISBN 978-1-6659-4281-2 (pbk)
ISBN 978-1-6659-4283-6 (ebook)

My name is Parker.
This is my papi and nana.

They live in another country called Portugal. I wish they had not moved so far away.

We walk through a big airport.

Then we board a big plane. "Ready for takeoff!" says the pilot.

We zip past puffy clouds and eat crunchy snacks.

Now it is time to sleep.
"Good night, teddy,"
says Cash.

When we land
Papi and Nana are
waiting for us.

"Welcome to Portugal!" they say.

At the new house Nana shows us her garden in the front yard.

In the backyard
we splash in the pool.

Later we explore the town. We walk along cobblestone streets to a shop filled with sweets.

I try a treat I have never eaten before. "Yum!" I say.

Today we board a big boat.
"Where are we going?"
I ask Papi.

He grins. "You will see," he says.

Our boat floats into a beautiful sea cave lit by the sun!

Afterward we go to a beach with water so crystal clear I can see my toes!

The next day we visit a castle in Spain! Spain is a country right next to Portugal.

The castle sits on top of a big hill.

"Make way for the queen!"
Ava declares.

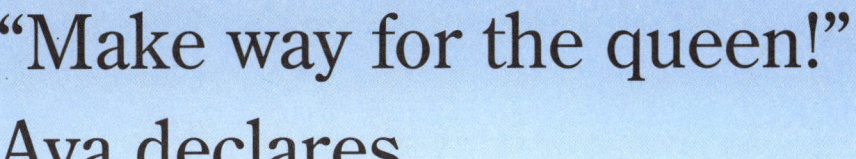

Now it is time to go home.
"Come visit us again!"
says Nana.

Visiting a new place with my family is so much fun!

CREATING AN ADVENTURE JOURNAL

Whether she is going on a long trip or somewhere special for the day, Parker is always up for an adventure. She loves to keep a journal where she can write about all the wonderful things that happened on her trip. You can try it too.

Before your next big adventure, write down where you are going and when you are going. How long will you be there? How are you getting there? Have you read any books or talked to anyone about the place you are going? What are you most excited to see or do?

When you are on your trip or when you get home, take some time to write about what you did. What was your favorite thing? Did you eat anything new or see something you've never seen before? Is there something special that you want to draw? Write down anything you want to remember.

Have fun and safe travels!